The Magic Griffle

and other stories

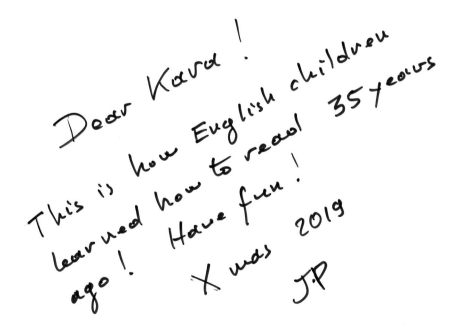

Dear Kava !

This is how English children learned how to read 35 years ago !. Have fun !

X mas 2019

J.P

Produced by Allegra Publishing Ltd, London
for Mercury Books Ltd
Editor : Felicia Law
Designer : Karen Radford

Published by
Mercury Junior an imprint of Mercury Books
20 Bloomsbury Street
London WC1B 3JH, UK

The Magic Griffle

and other stories

Sheila McCullagh

Illustrated by
Prue Theobalds, Tony Morris, Gavin Rowe,
John Dillow, Bookmatrix, India

Mercury Junior

The Griffle is a monster that lives in the Magician's garden at the end of Puddle Lane. The Griffle is a special kind of monster. It can vanish in bits. Sometimes you can only see its long green ears. Sometimes you can only see its big green eyes or its long green tail.

But whenever you do see it, there's bound to be a few surprises!

The Vanishing Monster

Davy and his sister Sarah lived in Puddle Lane. A Magician lived in Puddle Lane too. He lived in a big old house at the end of the lane. The house had a big garden where the children liked to play. Someone else lived in the garden too -

- and that "someone" was a Griffle!

One day, Davy pushed open the iron gate
and went into the Magician's garden.
The sun was shining and the sky was blue.
It was very hot. Davy had a strange
feeling. He felt that something
was there in the garden–
something he couldn't see!

Then he heard a strange noise, and
sat down under an old tree to listen.
It was an odd whiffly-griffly noise.

He hadn't been sitting there for very
long when he heard the sound again.
He looked up and saw two long
green ears floating in the air.
Suddenly there were two
green eyes under the
two green ears.

Davy sat very still and kept very
quiet. Soon he saw a long green
tail wriggle out of the bushes.

Davy was just a little bit frightened.
But he kept very quiet and he sat
very still. The ears and the eyes
and the tail came nearer
and nearer.

And then suddenly the ears and the eyes and the tail
all joined up together, and a big green monster came
out of the bushes and stood there, looking at Davy.

At that moment, Davy sneezed.
He couldn't help himself.
The sneeze burst out. "Attishoo!"

In a moment, the monster had
vanished! Davy didn't see it go.
It just wasn't there any more.
Davy stared.
The monster had gone.

"But it **WAS** there," he said,
"I didn't dream it."

Davy sat quite still and waited. (He didn't feel frightened any more. He was sure that the monster was more frightened then he was.)

Before long he saw two green ears again. Then he saw two green eyes - and then a long green tail.

The ears and the eyes were high up in the air.
"Please come back, monster," Davy said softly.

Then, as Davy watched, the ears and
the eyes and the tail all joined up together.
A big green monster, with a face a bit
like a lion, stood there on the grass
in front of him.

The monster's tail twitched
and its eyes were wide open.
It looked very nervous.

"Please don't be afraid, monster,"
said Davy. "I won't hurt you."

The monster jumped when Davy spoke.
For a moment, Davy thought that it
would vanish again. But it didn't.

It spoke in a whiffly-griffly voice.
"And I won't hurt you,"
said the monster.

"Who are you?" asked Davy.

"I'm a Griffle," said the monster,
in its whiffly-griffly voice.

"What's a Griffle?"
asked Davy.

"A Griffle is a vanishing
monster," said the
Griffle. "Griffles are
always being frightened
by people," it went on,
"so they always vanish
when they see anyone.
But I don't think I'm
frightened of you."

"Please don't be frightened of me," said Davy. "Stay here in the garden and play with me."

"Would you like to play at hide and seek?" asked the Griffle.

"But if you vanish, I shall never find you," said Davy.
"I'll leave a bit of me showing," said the Griffle.

16

So they played at hide and seek.
Davy hid first but the Griffle
soon found him. The Griffle
was very good at hiding.
All it had to do was vanish.

But it always left its ears
or its tail showing, so that
Davy could see it.

At last it was time for
Davy to go home.

"Please come with me,"
he said to the Griffle.
"I'd like you to come
and stay."

"You're sure you're
not frightened of me?"
asked the Griffle.

"I'm not a bit
frightened," said
Davy. "We've had
such a good game."

So Davy and the Griffle went
out of the garden together and made
their way back to Davy's house.

18

But as they got to the door
of Davy's house, Davy's sister
Sarah ran out.

"Hello Davy,"
she cried. "Where
have you been?"

"Sh!" said Davy.
"You'll frighten
the Griffle."

"But there's
no one here,"
said Sarah.

"Yes there is," said Davy.
"There's a Griffle."
"What's a Griffle?" asked Sarah.
"It's a monster," said Davy.
"But it's easily frightened
so you have to keep quiet"

And when Davy looked
the Griffle had vanished.

"It's gone," said Davy sadly.
"The Griffle was a friend
of mine and it's gone."

He didn't see the long
green tail by the door.

20

"There's nothing there," said Sarah. "You must be making it up."

"I'm not," said Davy. "It was here. It played with me in the garden. I wish it hadn't gone."

"Perhaps it'll come back," said Sarah.

"I will come back," a whiffly-griffly voice said softly. But the Griffle spoke so softly, the children didn't hear him.

21

The Griffle and Mr Gotobed

One day, Davy and Sarah were out playing
with their friends, Gita and Hari.
(Gita and Hari lived in Puddle Lane too.)

Sarah had a golden-coloured ball.
She tossed the ball to Gita and
Gita tossed the ball up high.

"Look out!" cried Davy.
"It's going through the window."
Davy was right.

They were playing outside
Mr Gotobed's house and his
bedroom window was wide
open. The ball went in
through the window.

"It's gone!" cried Sarah.

"It went through the window!"

"We must get it back," said Davy.

"We'll ask Mr Gotobed," said Hari.

"Mr Gotobed won't mind. He's very friendly. He'll throw it back."

Hari knocked on Mr Gotobed's door. Nothing happened.
He knocked again as hard as he could.

"I expect he's asleep," said Gita.

25

Gita was right. Mr Gotobed didn't
hear the knocking. As usual, he
was fast asleep in bed.

"He's fast asleep," said Sarah.
"What shall we do now? Grandmother
gave me the golden ball. She'll be very
sorry if we've lost it."

"We haven't lost it," said Gita.
"We know where it is. If Mr Gotobed
is asleep, we'll just have to wait
till he wakes up."

"But Grandmother is coming
to see us this afternoon,"
said Sarah. "I must have
it by then."

She knocked on Mr Gotobed's door.
She knocked as hard as she could.
But Mr Gotobed went on sleeping.
Sarah could hear him snoring

Suddenly Davy saw two green
ears sticking up over the wall
at the end of the lane.

"There's the Griffle!"
cried Davy. "The Griffle
will help us."

"Who's the Griffle?" asked Gita.
"The Griffle's a friend of mine,"
said Davy. "It's a vanishing monster.
Look! You can see its ears."

28

Two green eyes appeared under
the green ears.

"Please come and help us, Griffle,"
said Davy. "We were playing with
Sarah's ball, and her ball went
in at Mr Gotobed's window.
Mr Gotobed is fast asleep
and we can't get the
ball back."

The ears and eyes disappeared.
The gate into the garden opened
and closed, but they didn't see
anyone come through it.
And then suddenly there
was the Griffle! It was
standing in the lane.

Hari and Gita felt a bit frightened
at first, but they couldn't be
frightened for long. The Griffle
looked so friendly.

30

"What do you want me to do?"
it asked in a whiffly-griffly voice.
"You don't want me to go in
there, do you?"

"Please could you get the
ball back for us?" said Davy.
"It's Mr Gotobed's house.
He's fast asleep. He won't
see you."

"Well, I'll try," said the
Griffle. And it disappeared.

"It's gone!" said Gita.
"No, it hasn't," said Davy.
"It's only vanished.
Watch out for its ears."

The children looked at Mr Gotobed's house. Sarah saw two green ears outside Mr Gotobed's door.

"There it is!" she cried. The door opened and the two green ears disappeared inside the house.

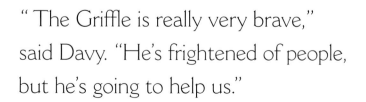

" The Griffle is really very brave," said Davy. "He's frightened of people, but he's going to help us."

Mr Gotobed was fast asleep in bed.
His mouth was open and he was
snoring gently.

Two green ears and two green eyes
looked inside the bedroom. Mr Gotobed
didn't see the bedroom door open softly
and the Griffle come in.

33

Mr Gotobed woke up. He sat up in bed.
He saw the Griffle and let out a yell.

"Aah!" cried Mr Gotobed.
"Help! There's a dragon
in my room."

"Help! Help! It's a dragon!
It must be a dragon!
But where is it now?"

The Griffle had vanished.

The Griffle **HAD** vanished.
But the Griffle hadn't gone.

Mr Gotobed got out of bed.
He went to the window.
He was so shaken that he
didn't see a beautiful golden ball
moving through the air towards
his bedroom door.

Mr Gotobed looked out of the window.
He saw Sarah and Gita, Hari and Davy,
down in the lane below.

"Have you seen a dragon?"
cried Mr Gotobed.
"No," said Davy. "We haven't."
"There aren't any dragons
in the lane," said Gita.
"There was a dragon
here in my bedroom!"
cried Mr Gotobed.

There was a big tree in the garden.
Sarah and Davy played in a big
hole in the old tree, but they
still didn't see the Griffle.
By now the Griffle wanted
to join in their game, but
he was just a bit nervous still.

When Davy climbed on a log,
the Griffle watched him
to make sure he didn't fall.
But still he didn't appear.

Sarah and Davy played by the house, but they
didn't see the Griffle. At last it was time
to go home. Sarah and Davy went out
of the gates and down the lane.

"I do wish I'd seen the Griffle,"
said Sarah.

"So do I," said Davy.

A dog lived in a house at the other end of the lane. He was a very big dog and he looked very fierce. Sarah and Davy liked most dogs but they didn't like this one.

As the two children went down the lane, the big dog looked out of the door of his house.

He saw Sarah and Davy
and ran up the lane towards
them, barking loudly.

He was barking because
he wanted to play, but
of course the children
didn't know this.

Sarah and Davy stopped.
They knew that they musn't run
or the dog would run after them!
But they felt a bit frightened.

The big dog ran up to them,
barking loudly.

"He won't harm us," said Sarah.
"No, he won't," said Davy,
"not if we stand still."

Suddenly, the dog stopped.
He let out a howl. His hair
went up. He looked up the
lane past Sarah and Davy.

His ears went down
and his tail went down.
It was the dog who
looked frightened now.

"What-what is it?" whispered Sarah.

The dog was staring at something behind them. Sarah and Davy turned round to look.
There was the Griffle!
The Griffle was standing in the middle of the lane.

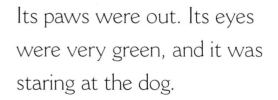

Its paws were out. Its eyes were very green, and it was staring at the dog.

The dog howled again.
He turned tail and ran
away as fast as he could.
He ran all the way back
down the lane with his
tail between his legs.

He ran into his house and
the door shut behind him
with a bang!

"You hide first," said the Griffle.

Sarah and Davy hid.
Sarah went behind the tree
and Davy hid in the bushes.

The Griffle didn't look
until they had hidden,
but he soon found them.

56

Then the Griffle hid.
The Griffle was very good
at hiding. They looked by the
steps and they looked behind
the tree, but they couldn't see
the Griffle.

Then Sarah saw a long green tail
coming out of the bushes. The Griffle
had left its tail showing so that Sarah
and Davy could see it.

"What are you doing,
Sarah?" asked
Mrs Pitter-Patter.

"I'm playing with
my friend," said Sarah.

"What friend?" asked Mrs Pitter-Patter.
"I'm playing with my friend the Griffle," said Sarah.
"What Griffle?" asked Mrs Pitter-Patter. "I can't see anyone."

60

"Look,"
said Sarah. "If you
look very hard, you can
see the Griffle's ears."

"What ears?"
said Mrs Pitter-Patter.
"I can only see two green leaves,"

The Griffle's green tail was hanging over
the wall. Mrs Pitter-Patter saw it.

"That's a green rope,"
said Mrs Pitter-Patter.

"But it isn't a rope," said Sarah.
"It's the Griffle's tail."

"Of course it's a rope,"
said Mrs Pitter-Patter.
"I shall pull it down!"

She took hold of the
Griffle's tail, and gave
it a long, hard pull.

"Gr-gr-grrrrr!"
The Griffle jumped down
from the wall with a roar!

As if by magic, the whole of the
Griffle was there. You could see
every bit of it standing on top
of the wall.

" Help!" cried Mrs Pitter-Patter
as she ran by. "A monster! Help! Help!"
"What is it?" cried Mr Gotobed.
"What's happened? Where are you
running to, Mrs Pitter-Patter?"

Mrs Pitter-Patter was running
so fast down the lane that
she didn't hear what
Mr Gotobed said.
She didn't even see him.

At last Mrs Pitter-Patter reached her own door.

She flung it open and ran into the house. She shut the door behind her with a bang!

"Yes, she's gone," said Sarah.
"Please come back and play."

Two green eyes appeared
under the green ears.
The Griffle looked
down the lane.

Mrs Pitter-Patter was
nowhere to be seen.

"She won't come back," said Sarah.
"All the same I think I'll come another
day when she isn't about,"
said the Griffle.

And with that, the ears and the eyes
disappeared and Sarah was alone!

The
Little Monster

Here's another story about the Griffle that lived in the garden of the old house in Puddle Lane. Although it could vanish when it wanted to, it was a little nervous.

But it liked to play with the children who lived in the lane.

Then it was the Griffle's turn to hide.
There was a very old tree in a corner
of the garden. The tree was
hollow. The Griffle hid
inside the hollow tree
and vanished.

But it left its tail showing
as it always did so that
Sarah could find it.

Sarah looked for the Griffle.
She looked in the bushes
and she looked by the house.
She crept round by a tree
but the Griffle wasn't there.

She looked by the
wall and she looked
by the gate. But she
didn't see the Griffle.

Sarah went towards the old tree.
She looked inside but she didn't
see the Griffle's tail lying
in the grass.

(The Griffle was green,
and so was its tail so it
didn't show up very well.)

Sarah had just gone past the tree
when she heard a great shout.
It was something like yell
and something like a roar.

"Aah! Ow! Grrr! Oooh!"

The yell came from the hollow tree.
Sarah ran back as fast as she could

She was just in time to see the Griffle.
It jumped out of the hollow tree
as if the tree was on fire!

"Oooh! Ow! Oooh!" it cried.

But the tree wasn't on
fire. It looked just as it
always did.

Sarah stood still, staring.
She couldn't see anything to be
afraid of. She looked at the tree
and she looked at the Griffle.

The Griffle landed on the
grass and turned to look at her.
It looked very frightened.

"Whatever is the matter, Griffle?"
asked Sarah.

The Griffle was shaking like a leaf.

"There's a m-m-monster
in the tree," said the Griffle,
"a little monster – a terrible
little monster!"

84

"What kind of monster?" asked Sarah. "I can't see any monster in the tree."

"I think you call it a m-m-mouse," said the Griffle.

She bent down and gently
picked up the little mouse.
She held it in her hands.

The Griffle shuddered

"I'll put it down in the lane,"
Sarah said, turning towards
the Griffle. "Then we can
go on playing."

"No, we can't," said the Griffle. "Where there is one mouse there are bound to be more. I'll come back another day."

And the Griffle vanished.

For a moment, Sarah saw two green ears behind a bush. Then the Griffle was gone.

Sarah looked at the little mouse.
It didn't seem to be at all frightened.
It sat on Sarah's hand.
It looked very thin.

"I'll take you home,"
said Sarah. "I'll find
some cheese for you."

She put the little
mouse in her pocket,
and went out of the
gate into Puddle Lane.
She kept one hand
on the mouse so that
it wouldn't jump out.

She hadn't gone very far
when she met Mrs Pitter-Patter.

"Sarah," said Mrs Pitter-Patter,
"Take your hand out of your
pocket. You should never walk
along with your hands
in your pocket."

"But I have a mouse in my pocket,
Mrs Pitter-Patter," said Sarah.
"Look! I am taking him home."

She took the little mouse
out of her pocket and
opened her hand.

Mrs Pitter-Patter screamed almost as loudly
as the Griffle had roared. She jumped
in the air and turned around. She ran
home down Puddle Lane as fast
as she could.

Sarah and the little
mouse stared after her.

"She must be afraid of mice too," said Sarah.

She looked at the little mouse. It was sitting on her hand and combing its whiskers with its paws. It didn't seem to mind Sarah at all.

"I don't know why anyone
would be afraid of you,"
said Sarah. "I'll take you
home and give you some
supper. Then I'll put you
back in the old tree."

And she did.